# TERROR IN CUBICLE FOUR

The door to the girls' toilets opened slowly, and James cautiously took a step inside.

'What's the matter?' asked Alexander, forcing the door wide and pushing past him. 'Scared something might bite you?'

'No,' answered James, 'it's just that I've never been inside the girls' toilets before.'

Suddenly, the loo inside the closed cubicle let out a loud burp, and Lenny backed away from the door. 'Leandra says that one's the haunted one,' he muttered.

Alexander laughed. 'A haunted toilet is a scientific impossibility.'

But the words stuck in his throat as the toilet let out another enormous belch. James gasped as a withered, grey human hand launched itself up from the water, and landed on his face.

## St Sebastian's School in Grimesford is the pits. No, really – it is.

Every year, the high school sinks a bit further into the boggy plague pit beneath it and, every year, the ghosts of the plague victims buried underneath it become a bit more cranky.

Egged on by their spooky ringleader, Edith Codd, they decide to get their own back – and they're willing to play dirty. *Really* dirty.

They kick up a stink by causing as much mischief as in inhumanly possible so as to get St Sebastian's closed down once and for all.

But what they haven't reckoned on is year-seven new boy, James Simpson and his friends Alexander and Lenny.

The question is, are the gang up to the challenge of laying St Sebastian's paranormal problem to rest, or will their school remain forever frightful?

**There's only one way to find out . . .**

**www.too-ghoul.com**

# TERROR IN CUBICLE FOUR

## B. STRANGE

### EGMONT

Special thanks to:

Tommy Donbavand, St John's Walworth Church of
England Primary School and Belmont Primary School

# EGMONT

*We bring stories to life*

Published in Great Britain 2007
by Egmont UK Limited
239 Kensington High Street, London W8 6SA

Text & illustrations © 2007 Egmont UK Ltd
Text by Tommy Donbavand
Illustrations by Pulsar Studio (Beehive Illustration)

ISBN 978 1 4052 3233 3

3 5 7 9 10 8 6 4

A CIP catalogue record for this title is available
from the British Library

Typeset by Avon DataSet Ltd, Bidford on Avon, Warwickshire
Printed and bound in Great Britain by the CPI Group

'More books – I love it!'
**Ashley, age 11**

'It's disgusting. . .'
**Joe, age 10**

'. . . it's all good!'
**Alexander, age 9**

'. . . loads of excitement and really gross!'
**Jay, age 9**

'I like the way there's the brainy boy,
the brawny boy and the cool boy that form
a team of friends'
**Charlie, age 10**

'That ghost Edith is wicked'
**Matthew, age 11**

'This is really good and funny!'
**Sam, age 9**

# School versus...

Year-seven new boy
and chief spook-hunter

**James Simpson**

Headmaster's son
and official brainiac

**Alexander Tick**

Strong as an ox,
gentle as an
unusually tall lamb

**Lenny Maxwell**

# ...Ghoul!

Loud-mouthed ringleader of the plague-pit ghosts

Edith Codd

Young ghost and a secret wannabe St Sebastian's pupil

William Scroggins

Bone idle ex-leech merchant with a taste for all things gross

Ambrose Harbottle

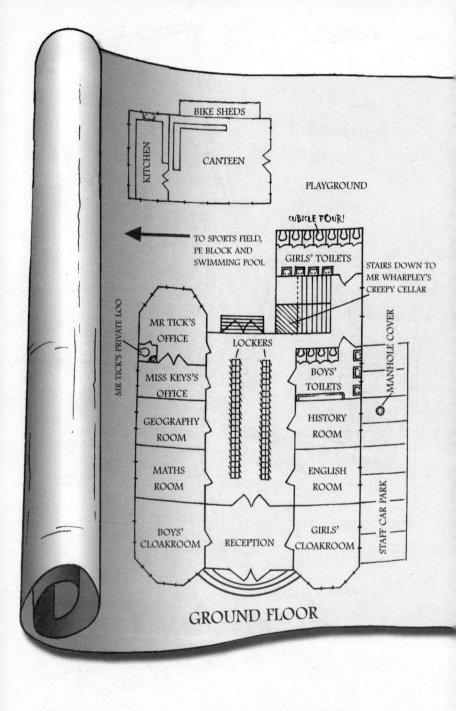

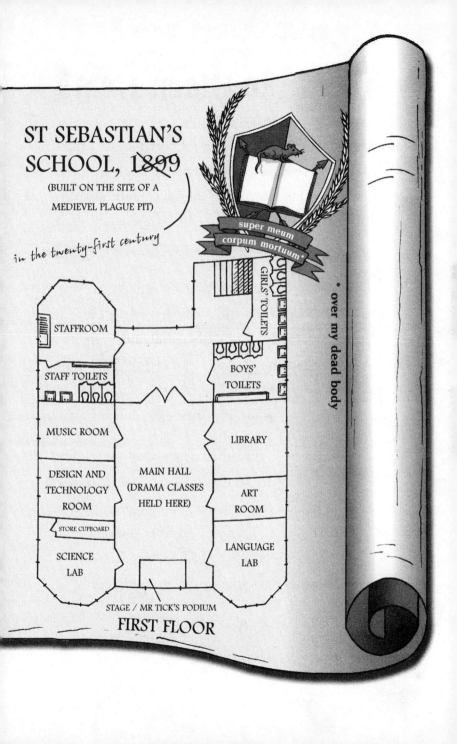

# About the Black Death

**The Black Death** was a terrible plague that
is believed to have been spread by fleas on rats.
It swept through Europe in the fourteenth century,
arriving in England in 1348, where it killed
over one third of the population.

One of the Black Death's main symptoms was
**foul-smelling boils all over the body called
'buboes'.** The plague was so infectious that its
victims and their families were locked in their houses
until they died. Many villages were abandoned as
the disease wiped out their populations.

So many people died that graveyards overflowed
and bodies lay in the street, so special **'plague pits'**
were dug to bury the bodies. Almost every town
and village in England has a plague pit
somewhere underneath it, so watch out
when you're digging in the garden . . .

Dear Reader

As you may have already guessed, B. Strange is not a real name.

The author of this series is an ex-teacher who is currently employed by a little-known body called the Organisation For Spook Termination (Excluding Demons), or O.F.S.T.(E.D.). 'B. Strange' is the pen name chosen to protect his identity.

Together, we felt it was our duty to publish these books, in an attempt to save innocent lives. The stories are based on the author's experiences as an O.F.S.T.(E.D.) inspector in various schools over the past two decades.

Please read them carefully - you may regret it if you don't . . .

Yours sincerely
The Publisher.


PS - Should you wish to file a report on any suspicious supernatural occurrences at your school, visit **www.too-ghoul.com** and fill out the relevant form. We'll pass it on to O.F.S.T.(E.D.) for you.

PPS - All characters' names have been changed to protect the identity of the individuals. Any similarity to actual persons, living or undead, is purely coincidental.

# CONTENTS

| 1 | FEELING FLUSHED | 1 |
| 2 | A BIG HAND | 12 |
| 3 | GOING UNDERGROUND | 22 |
| 4 | GHOUL'S OUT | 32 |
| 5 | BEST CELLAR | 41 |
| 6 | THE BLUEPRINT | 51 |
| 7 | THE WHOLE TRUTH? | 60 |
| 8 | RAT FANS | 68 |
| 9 | WHARPLEY ON THE WARPATH | 78 |
| 10 | WORSE | 89 |
| 11 | A TENTS SITUATION | 100 |
| 12 | BULLY BAITING | 109 |
| 13 | SKY HIGH | 119 |
| | EXTRA! FACT FILE, JOKES, QUIZ AND STUFF | 131 |
| | THE BUBONIC BUILDERS SNEAK PREVIEW | 137 |

# CHAPTER 1
# FEELING FLUSHED

'No, I can't fill in the remaining three wives of Henry the Eighth myself!' roared Gordon as he pushed Alexander's head into the toilet bowl and flushed for the second time. 'I want the headmaster's son to do it for me!'

James Simpson leapt forwards and managed to grab a handful of the bully's shirt before the heel of a hand pushed into his face and sent him sprawling across the greasy floor of the boys' toilets. Lenny Maxwell dashed over to help him up.

'We have to do something!' hissed James, rubbing his bruised nose. 'If Mr Tick gets wind that we were in here when this happened to his son, we'll be in detention for the rest of our natural lives.'

Lenny nodded. 'Right!' he said, more to himself than to anyone else. 'Here I go, doing something! I'm going to do something!'

Alexander's head appeared from the toilet bowl after his third flushing. 'Step in any time you want, boys!' he cried out.

Lenny took a cautious pace towards the bully, and immediately pulled back.

'What's wrong?' asked James.

'A plan,' mumbled Lenny, 'I need a plan.'

Alexander came up for the fourth time. 'You don't need a plan!' he screamed. 'Just *do* something!'

Lenny cracked his neck from side to side as James busily rubbed his shoulders. 'You're a bully-fighting machine!' James told him. 'A giant of a man! You're a contender!'

'A contender!' repeated the giant of a man.

Alexander reappeared briefly. 'In your own time, Lenny. Don't mind me!'

Lenny took a deep breath and drew himself up to his full 1.7-metre height. He clamped a hand on Gordon's chest and spun him round.

'What?' the bully spat, his nose just centimetres from Lenny's chin.

'Leave him alone, Carver,' said Lenny, as calmly as he could. He gripped the bully's jumper even tighter in an attempt to disguise his trembling hand. 'He's already done your maths and science homework this week. I'd have thought even a numpty like you could look up a little bit of history and copy it out for himself.'

The expression that flooded Gordon 'The Gorilla' Carver's face was something Lenny had only seen before on nature programmes: pure, animal rage. Behind him, Alexander clambered unsteadily to his feet, shaking his head in an effort to clear the dizziness.

'I'll give you three seconds to let go of me, Maxwell,' growled the bully. 'Or it'll be your fat head that gets flushed next!' Drops of stinking toilet water splashed across the back of Gordon's neck and, realising that Alexander was now standing, he reached out and grabbed the boy's face, pushing him back down towards the toilet bowl once again. 'Did I give you permission to get up, Stick?'

'Leave him ALONE!' yelled Lenny, stepping backwards and pulling The Gorilla out of the cubicle with him. There was a ripping sound, and both boys looked down to see the torn St Sebastian's School badge in Lenny's fist. A gaping hole of the same shape decorated Gordon's jumper.

Silence filled the toilets as all three of his victims held their breath.

'Mummy!' muttered Lenny, the first to speak. 'I . . . I didn't mean . . .'

The Gorilla sprang forwards and grabbed Lenny by the throat, pushing him back over the row of sinks that lined the far wall, his head pressed hard against the one remaining mirror. 'Do you have any idea what my dad will do to me for this?' he shouted, slamming Lenny back against the graffiti-covered glass. 'Give me your jumper!' With his free hand, Gordon began to pull Lenny's jumper up over his head.

James and Alexander glanced nervously at each other, then raced to help. They grabbed Carver's shoulders and tried to pull him off their struggling friend, but the bully was too strong. James jumped on to The Gorilla's back and wrestled him backwards, only collapsing to the floor when a well-aimed elbow crashed into his stomach and took the wind out of him.

Lenny's jumper was halfway over his head when a scream rang out. At first, James thought Alexander had been hit, maybe punched in the face – but, as he used the ageing iron radiator to pull himself to his feet, he realised that the sound had come from next door. From the girls' toilets.

Gordon froze at the sound, just long enough for Lenny to wriggle free of his grip and pull his jumper back down. Another scream echoed out, and James took his chance, stepping directly in front of the bully.

'Ms Legg will have heard that,' he said. 'She's on duty today. She'll be here any minute. You want her to see this?'

Gordon Carver struggled to catch his breath. 'I'll be back for that jumper!' he snarled, pointing menacingly at Lenny. He reached out and snatched his torn school badge from the boy's hand, then dashed out of the toilets, pausing to spit a gobful of phlegm at Alexander before disappearing through the door.

'Are you OK?' asked James.

Lenny slumped against the wall and nodded silently, trying in vain to reshape his badly stretched jumper. There was a mechanical whirr as the hand dryer clicked in to action and Alexander stuck his head underneath it, rubbing furiously at his spit-covered hair.

'Thanks for the help,' he shouted over the noise of the machine, 'but it wasn't necessary. I could have handled Carver myself.'

'Yeah, of course you could,' replied James. 'You were just keeping your face down in the toilet bowl until you found the perfect time to strike.'

'Not handled like *that*,' said Alexander. 'I'd simply have put in his homework that Henry VIII's last three wives were called Daphne, Melissa and Chantelle. He'd have got into serious trouble for that.'

James nodded. 'And you'd have been on his hit list for the next ten years. I tell you, something's got to –'

Another noise interrupted him – this time not a scream, but the sound of a girl crying.

James, Alexander and Lenny stepped out of the ground-floor boys' toilets to find a crowd of year-eight girls outside the girls' toilets across the passageway. At the centre of the group was Stacey Carmichael, sobbing and trembling as her friends tried to calm her. Lenny spotted his older sister – and Stacey's best friend – Leandra, among the crowd and pulled her to one side.

'What's going on?' he asked. 'Was Stacey the one who was screaming?'

Leandra nodded. 'She was in one of the toilet cubicles, trying on her new ballet pumps and just lost it! Something must have happened in there.'

'Like what?' asked James.

'No idea,' shrugged Leandra. 'We haven't been able to get a word out of her.'

'I'd better find out so that I can tell my dad,' announced Alexander and, before James could stop him, he pushed his way through the group of girls. When he got to Stacey, he stopped and stared. She was wearing new ballet pumps but, along with everything below the hem of her ridiculously short school skirt, they were covered in lumpy, green slime. 'What happened?' asked Alexander.

Stacey looked up at him through red, tear-filled eyes and fought to hold back her sobs. 'The t-toilet!' she mumbled. 'It j-just threw up over m-me!' She pulled a handful of tissues from her school bag and tried unsuccessfully to clean her legs; the slime simply spread further across her skin. 'My new b-ballet pumps are ruined!' She began crying again.

Leandra pushed through and put an arm around Stacey's shoulders, staying clear of the

gunk that was now oozing on to the floor of the passageway.

Alexander looked up. James and Lenny were now standing with him. 'Stacey,' he said, gravely, 'which toilet cubicle were you in?'

Stacey looked up again, tears streaming down her face. 'C-cubicle four!' she sobbed.

## CHAPTER 2
# A BIG HAND

The door to the girls' toilets opened slowly, and James cautiously took a step inside.

'What's the matter?' asked Alexander, forcing the door wide and pushing past him. 'Scared something might bite you?'

'No,' answered James, 'it's just that I've never been inside the girls' toilets before.'

'Me neither,' added Lenny.

'Well, *I've* been in here *loads* of times,' boasted Alexander. 'Being the headmaster's son does have some advantages, you know!'

Lenny opened his mouth to ask what the advantage to having access to the girls' toilets might be, but James silenced him with a single shake of his head. They followed their eager friend through the door, letting it swing shut behind them.

James studied the room. It was just like the boys' toilets, except the cubicles were on the opposite side to the door, and the walls were

13

painted in a violent pink instead of the murky grey that greeted the male pupils each day.

'Phew, I hope it didn't smell like that when she ate it!' said Lenny, pinching his nose closed and screwing up his face.

'What?' asked James, sniffing the air before suddenly wishing he hadn't. The stench was overpowering.

'Whatever Stacey Carmichael was producing in cubicle four!' replied Lenny, trying not to take a breath.

Alexander shook his head earnestly. 'That's not a human odour,' he said, flicking his tongue out as though trying to taste the smell. 'Human faeces has a nitrogen and sulphur base, while this aroma has a metallic tinge, as though there's some kind of magnesium compound at work.'

'You what?' asked Lenny through clenched lips.

'He means, that ain't no normal poo,' explained James. He turned to Alexander.

14

'Remember we talked about you getting out more often? Not working, is it?'

'Shh!' commanded Alexander. 'Quiet!'

All three boys stopped where they were and listened hard. A faint bubbling sound could be heard . . . and it was coming from cubicle four.

'That'll be where your geranium smell's coming from then,' said Lenny, prodding at the cubicle door with his foot.

'Magnesium, not geranium!' sighed Alexander. 'We covered all this stuff in science at least three weeks ago. Don't you ever listen to a word Mr Watts says?'

Lenny simply shrugged, and pulled his misshapen jumper up over his face to try and combat the stink.

'Well, go on then!' said James to Alexander, pushing him towards the cubicle door.

'Why me?' asked Alexander. 'There's no reason why it has to be me who goes in there.'

'You're the one who knows all about this stuff. You just told us, remember, Einstein?'

'About the chemical make-up of the smell, certainly,' argued Alexander. 'But if there's someone – or some*thing* – in there, I think I've proved conclusively that I'm the least capable at handling that type of scenario!'

'Some*thing*?' said James. 'What do you think is in there? The Bogeyman?'

'I don't know what's in there,' replied Alexander, 'none of us does. But in case it's one of The Gorilla's cronies messing about, or someone else that needs physically manhandling, I think it should be Lenny who goes in first.'

'*What?*' cried Lenny, spinning round to stop Alexander from hiding behind him. 'Why *me*?'

'You're the biggest,' explained Alexander. 'The muscle to my mind. The brawn to my brains.'

'What does that make me?' asked James.

Alexander shrugged. 'You're the looks.'

'Thanks,' mumbled James.

The toilet inside the closed cubicle let out a loud burp, and Lenny backed away from the door. 'I think James should go in first!' he said.

'What, and risk spoiling these looks? No *way!*'

'Honestly. There's nothing to be worried about,' said Alexander. 'The toilet simply hasn't been maintained in the correct manner by Mr Wharpley. The drains have backed up and, when Stacey tried to flush, the pipes spewed a handful of waste over her precious ballet pumps. Being girls, they just made a big deal out of it.'

'I don't know,' muttered Lenny. 'Leandra says that one's the haunted toilet.'

Alexander laughed. 'A haunted toilet is a scientific impossibility. The existence of an afterlife has yet to be proven and, should life after death ever be shown to be a reality, I seriously doubt it would locate itself beyond the U-bend of a school toilet.'

'Well, go and have a look then!' said Lenny.

'No chance!'

James turned away from the mirror, where he'd been examining his newly discovered looks. 'You know, we could always just *tell* the girls we went in there . . .'

'What do you mean?' asked Alexander.

'Simple,' replied James. 'We just go out there and tell them we stormed the cubicle, faced down whatever was in there, and emerged triumphant.'

'A deception?' pondered Alexander. 'That would definitely go some way to enhancing my image around the school.'

'And it would certainly impress Stacey Carmichael, wouldn't it, Romeo?' said Lenny, nudging James repeatedly on the arm.

James blushed a shade of pink that almost matched the toilet walls. 'I don't know what you're talking about!' he mumbled.

18

'Then it's settled!' announced Alexander.
'We go back outside, and proclaim victory!'

As the three boys turned to leave the room, the main door swung open. Stacey and Leandra stepped inside.

'Well?' asked Stacey.

'Well what?' said James, carefully avoiding eye contact with her.

'What happened when you went into the cubicle?' asked Leandra.

Alexander walked forwards, oozing what he believed was charm. 'It was a tremendous skirmish. We battled a mutant being comprised entirely of waste materials, ripping and tearing at its rancid, engorged body. However, we stood our ground, defeated the creature, and the facility is now safe for use again.'

Stacey remained expressionless. 'So, you haven't been in there at all?' she said.

James shook his head. 'No, not even a peek.'

Alexander folded his arms and sighed. 'What did you say that for? We had them, then!'

'We're not as dumb as you look, Stick boy!' said Leandra. 'Now, get in that cubicle and see what's happening.'

James looked from Alexander to Lenny and back again. Then, realising that neither one was going to move, he took a deep breath. 'All right! I suppose I'll have to do it!'

He strode over to cubicle four, closed his eyes tightly and pushed the door open. After a second, when no one had come rushing out at him, he opened his eyes and looked inside. The cubicle was empty and, apart from the fact that the water in the toilet bowl was bubbling slightly, everything looked fine.

'See!' he said. 'I *told* you there was nothing to worry about!'

But the words stuck in his throat as the toilet let out another enormous belch. James gasped as a withered, grey human hand launched itself up from the water, and landed on his face.

# CHAPTER 3
# GOING UNDERGROUND

There was a brief moment of quiet before
Stacey's scream pierced the silence. James
scrambled to pull the rotting hand from his face,
convinced that the fingers would make a grab
for his throat at any moment. Ripping it away
from his mouth, he flung the severed limb as far
as he could across the room. It hit the wall with
a 'splat' and slowly slid to the floor, leaving a
sticky trail of goo behind it.

Everyone ran for the main door at the same
time, and Leandra managed to fall to the floor.

Alexander tripped over her, pulling James and
Stacey down with him. Lenny stooped to help
them up, but stopped as he spotted something
out of the corner of his eye. A long, purple
tentacle, covered in suckers, was rising from the
water of the toilet bowl in cubicle four.

23

It stretched upwards towards the ceiling, elongating as though glad to be free of the confining pipes and then dropped to the floor, where it dragged itself towards the group of children.

Stacey screamed again and tried to back away, but Alexander was lying across her legs, and she found it impossible to move at all. Leandra scrambled to her feet and pulled Alexander off her friend, allowing Stacey to shuffle backwards towards the door.

Flat on his back, James could only watch in terror as the tentacle crept steadily towards him, its tip raised as if to sniff the air and navigate its way across the room. As the first slimy sucker touched James's ankle, Lenny leapt forwards and pulled his friend away from the creeping feeler.

James launched himself at the main door at the same time as Stacey and Leandra, the trio getting jammed momentarily before collapsing out into the passageway, Lenny and Alexander falling on top of them as they quickly followed.

The door to the girls' toilets closed softly, and the group lay together for a moment, trying to catch their breath. Only when James realised that his arm was draped across Stacey's chest did he stand up and move away.

'What the flip was that?' he asked, as he sank down on to the bottom step of the nearby staircase.

'Which one do you mean?' replied Leandra. 'The dead hand, or the slimy tentacle?'

'Did that really just happen?' said Alexander.

'Well, I'm not going back in to find out!' said Lenny.

Suddenly, Alexander leapt to his feet, a horrified look on his face. 'Oh, no!' he cried.

James raised a hand and gently patted his friend's back. 'Don't worry,' he said. 'It's just the shock kicking in.'

'Not that!' shouted Alexander. 'We're late for science! And it's chemical reactions today!' He grabbed his school bag, and raced off down the corridor in the direction of Mr Watts's classroom.

Lenny shook his head as Alexander disappeared, then helped his sister and Stacey to their feet, and picked up his own bag. 'I'll see you later,' he said, stumbling after his class-mate in a daze.

Stacey leant forwards and rubbed at the now-dried slime that covered her legs. 'This stuff is starting to burn a bit,' she moaned.

Leandra exchanged looks with James, then wrapped an arm around Stacey's shoulders. 'I'd better help her get her cleaned up.'

James nodded and watched as they trudged off down the corridor. With a final glance at the door to the girls' toilets, he hoisted his rucksack on to his shoulder and set off to be baffled by chemical reactions.

Alexander was busy writing about why an atom cannot be broken down without altering the chemical nature of its substance when a ball of paper landed in front of him. Carefully checking that Mr Watts was still facing the board, he opened the note and read the simple sentence within: What are we going to do? He nudged James, who snapped himself out of whatever terrible daydream he was suffering, and studied the note.

'What should I put?' asked Alexander in a whisper. James looked three rows back to see Lenny, waiting eagerly for a reply.

'We'll have to go back in there,' said James, taking the note from his friend and beginning to write. Alexander snatched the piece of paper back from him.

'Are you *crazy*? We can't go back in there! If anything, we have to tell my dad.'

'Tell him what, exactly?' hissed James. 'That a monster tried to attack us in the girls' toilets? He'd have us locked up.'

'I'll show him the hand,' said Alexander. 'That'll still be there, even if the tentacle isn't.'

'Don't be stupid!' snapped James. 'That's just asking for trouble. If your dad gets involved, we'll be cross-examined for weeks about why we were mucking about in there. He's bound to think it's some sort of practical joke. Either that, or we've gone totally insane!'

A voice cut into their conversation. 'I hope today's chemistry lesson isn't interrupting your social life, Mr Simpson . . .' said Mr Watts.

James blushed and shook his head. 'No, sir,' he replied. 'Alexander was just explaining something about atoms to me.'

'Well, do it quietly,' ordered Mr Watts before turning back to the board and continuing with his diagram of electrons.

When the ball of paper finally landed back on Lenny's desk, it contained one simple instruction: Meet behind the bike sheds at lunchtime.

Alexander was the first to reach the meeting point, having wolfed down a couple of energy bars as he dashed across the playground. James arrived a few moments later, shortly before Lenny appeared, tucking into a bag of fish and chips.

'How can you think of eating at a time like this?' asked Alexander.

Lenny shrugged. 'Dunno. Just hungry.'

James ignored them both. 'Right,' he said, 'we're all agreed that involving adults at this stage won't do us any good at all.'

Alexander started to argue, but James held up a hand to silence him. 'It won't help, I promise you. There was a kid at my old school who claimed he'd seen a UFO, and they sent him off to some child psychologist every Thursday for six months.'

A grin spread across Alexander's face. 'Were his appointments after school, or did he have to go at *launch*time?' he asked.

Lenny sighed. 'Is that from your computer database of jokes?' he asked.

Alexander nodded enthusiastically. 'What do you think?'

'You need a hard-drive crash!' said Lenny.

James interrupted. 'Stop it, you two! We've got to find out what kind of creature that tentacle belongs to.'

'How are we supposed to do that?' asked Lenny through a mouthful of cod.

James simply shrugged, lost for an answer. Alexander thought for a moment, then spoke up. 'It's a water-based animal, whatever it is. Much like that fish you're eating.'

Lenny spat out the remaining bits of fish and dumped his lunch into the nearest bin. 'Thanks a lot!' he said.

'If we can turn off the water supply,' continued Alexander, unaware, 'it will have to leave the toilets in search of another home, and we should be able to track it.'

'How do we turn off the water?' asked James.

Alexander smiled. 'We go to the basement!'

## CHAPTER 4
# GHOUL'S OUT

'Order! Order!' yelled Edith Codd, banging
a human skull repeatedly on to an upturned
barrel. 'I insist upon order, or there will be no
surface passes handed out this Halloween
whatsoever!'

Reluctantly, over a thousand men, women and
children stopped their nattering and turned their
attentions towards Edith. She sighed heavily; this
job would be the death of her. If she hadn't
already been dead for over six hundred years,
of course.

'Ambrose Harbottle, are you chewing?' she quizzed, leaning over the top of her barrel. The middle-aged ghost glanced around casually before realising with horror that Edith was talking to him.

'Mmm-mm!' he mumbled, shaking his head, then he pretended to cough and slipped the juicy leech out of his mouth as silently as he could. Beside him, a young ghoul sniggered noisily and nudged his fellow spirit in the ribs.

'She got you!' he teased.

'William Scroggins! One hundred lines: I must not mock fellow members of the walking deceased!' bellowed Edith.

'Aw!' moaned William. 'I was going to play catch with the Headless Horseman after this, as well!'

Edith took a deep breath and gazed around the enormous underground cavern constructed painstakingly over the past six centuries by the ghosts and ghouls in front of her. What had once been a school sewer system was now an amphitheatre of incredible proportions. If only the assembled legions of the undead would appreciate it.

'First order of business,' began Edith, as efficiently as she could given the circumstances. 'I think we would all like to thank Lady Grimes for her ectoplasm-renewal workshop last week. I know a lot of you attended, and the benefits are obvious, as many of you don't look a day over three hundred as a result.'

Lady Grimes stood to receive a smattering of bored applause.

'Next, I am saddened to announce that the bones of our dear departed selves have been tampered with again! May I remind you that we died from the Black Death, people, and that disturbing the unmarked graves into which we were tossed without ceremony will do little if anything to help the environment.' Edith sighed again. 'It's bad enough that we have to deal with ghostal warming, without some prankster building goalposts from the spines of plague victims.'

A barely disguised laugh echoed from the back of the hall, and Edith glared in its direction. 'And don't think I don't know what you did with my former ribs, Bertram Ruttle! It's not big and it's not clever – even if it is musical.'

A wave of chatter spread through the amphitheatre again, and Edith was forced to hammer the skull down once more. To the amusement of William, it shattered into a hundred pieces although Edith, ignoring her own orders about disturbing graves, simply dug her hand down into the soil and pulled up another to use. A tiny voice to the left was heard to cry out: 'Hey, that's me!'

'Order! Order!' Edith's wafer-thin patience was wearing down even further. The closest thing to silence she was likely to get eventually prevailed. 'And, our final item on the agenda –'

Suddenly, Edith was interrupted by the ringing of a muffled bell from above. Every ghost in the cavern raised its eyes towards the roof of the sewer as a thousand pairs of children's feet hit the floor at the same time and began to clatter about. The noise was tremendous, and bits of old pipe rained down upon the crowd, turning a number of phantoms into little more than puddles of spectral goo.

'– St Sebastian's School!' growled Edith as she finished her sentence unheard. Thankfully, it was lunchtime, and the din subsided slightly as most of the children headed outside to the playground.

'As you know, Ambrose Harbottle has been working hard on what he likes to call "Terror in Cubicle Four", otherwise know to the rest of us as "Operation Stupid Purple Tentacle!" '

'That's not fair!' yelled Ambrose, angrily. 'It took all my energy to transform into that tentacle, *and* I managed to scare at least five pupils!' He folded his arms, sulking. 'There's a trio of children who won't be weeing into *that* particular toilet for the foreseeable future!'

'As successful as you consider your plan to have been, Ambrose, the simple truth is that it hasn't worked,' responded Edith. 'The school is still open. We'll have to scare more than three pupils in order to get it closed down.'

She gazed from blank face to blank face in the audience before her. 'Do you want this racket to continue after every single lesson? Shall we just sit here and wait until the foundations of the school collapse in on us? Are our remains not precious and sacred?'

As if to underscore the speech, Bertram Ruttle picked out a military march on the xylophone he'd constructed from Edith's ribs.

'These children need a good fright, people!
We must frighten them with the leeches, we must
frighten them in the classrooms and in the lab.
Give us the ghouls, and we will finish the job!'

Edith's eyes glowed red as her passion grew
and, for the first time in history, all the plague-
pit ghosts – with the exception of William and
Ambrose – were being carried along with her.

This was her moment. This was when she would begin the downfall of St Sebastian's School. 'Ask not what your tomb can do for you for, but what you can do for your tomb!'

The ghosts were already on their feet, applauding wildly as she struck a pose and cried out, 'Go forth and terrify!'

As a swell of pride and enthusiasm washed away centuries of indifference, Edith Codd pointed a bony finger at the spirit of the young farm boy who had been cut down by the Black Death at the tender age of eleven.

'William Scroggins,' she screamed. 'You're going to the surface!'

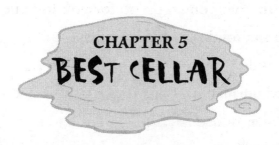

## CHAPTER 5
# BEST CELLAR

'First the girls' toilets, now the basement,'
muttered Lenny. 'I'm visiting all sorts of exotic
new places today.'

'Technically it's not a basement, it's a cellar,'
Alexander corrected. 'A basement would be a
purposely constructed room, whereas this area
will have been the storage vault, excavated from
the foundations of the original school building.'

'Do you think there'll come a day when you
get sick of the sound of your own voice?'
asked Lenny.

'I doubt it,' retorted Alexander.

'Will you two stop bickering?' hissed James as he led the way down the stairs and into the dark ahead, the faint glow of his mobile-phone screen barely lighting the way. 'The last thing we need is Mr Wharpley on the warpath.'

'I agree,' added Alexander. 'The man's a liability. How he got the job of school caretaker with those multiple murder convictions on his record is beyond me.'

'M-murder convictions?' stammered Lenny.

'Oh, yeah,' said Alexander. 'I saw his file in my dad's office once. They never found two of the bodies . . .'

'I have to go back up,' muttered Lenny, swallowing hard as James turned the screen of his mobile to face him. 'I, er . . . forgot to get my science homework from Mr Watts.'

Lenny had made it halfway up the staircase by the time James caught his arm. 'He's winding you up, you idiot!' he said. 'Now, let's just turn the water supply off, and we can get out of here.'

Lenny followed James and Alexander down to the large cellar, where the boys found a light switch and flicked it on. A dirty, low-wattage bulb flared into life, relieving little of the gloom.

'Right,' said Alexander. 'What now?'

James shrugged. 'It might surprise you to know that, seeing as I'm not yet a fully qualified plumber, I've never switched off a water supply before.' He scanned the network of pipes that ran along the walls. 'I suppose there must be some sort of tap to turn, but it could take us ages to find it.'

'We should split up,' suggested Alexander, much to Lenny's horror.

'Split up?' he muttered. 'I don't like the sound of that!'

'I agree,' said Alexander. 'There could be anything down here,' he teased.

43

James punched his arm angrily. 'Will you pack it in about Mr Wharpley?' he said, gesturing to Lenny as his friend grew pale. 'If he faints, I don't fancy lugging him back up those stairs!'

Alexander rubbed his dead arm, a stern expression on his face. 'I'm not *talking* about Mr Wharpley,' he explained. 'In case you're forgetting, there's a creature with long, purple tentacles wandering about, accompanied by someone who's short one very dead, severed hand!'

There was a brief moment of silence while all three boys let this information settle in, broken eventually by James.

'We haven't got time to worry about that,' he said. 'If we don't get a move on we'll be discovered. Now, let's look for a way to turn off the water.' He gestured to a doorway to his left. 'Lenny, you take that room. Alexander can do in here, and I'll search through the archway over

there. If we follow the pipes along the wall we're bound to find something.'

As James finished speaking, he became aware of a rumbling sound that slowly grew in volume, becoming louder and louder until it seemed to envelop the cellar. Before long, it was accompanied by a banging and clanking so noisy that it forced the boys to hold their hands over their ears. Lenny looked as though he might wet himself.

'The tentacle's back!' he screamed. 'It's coming for us!'

Alexander dashed over to the wall, and pressed his hands in turn against a series of the old, metal pipes. 'It's the waste supply,' he shouted over the din. 'Someone's flushed a toilet above us.' He pointed to the two unsearched rooms. 'Follow the pipes now! Ignore any that you can feel water running through; they're going in the wrong direction. The remaining pipes will feed water up to the school. The tap will be somewhere along one of those.'

Reluctantly, Lenny ran for the door at the far end of the cellar. Taking a deep breath, he turned the handle and pushed, praying for the door to be locked, but it swung open on aged, rusty hinges.

He found himself inside a workshop, filled to the brim with tools, broken desks and boxes of screws. This was obviously where Mr Wharpley spent most of his caretaking day. Hearing that the noise from the pipes was beginning to subside, Lenny gently touched each one in turn until he found one that lacked the vibration of the others, and began to follow it along the wall.

After a few metres, it disappeared behind a large, metal shelving unit, packed with more tools than Lenny had ever seen in one place. *If Mr Wharpley's got all these screwdrivers,* he mused, *how come the sports-hall noticeboard has been hanging off the wall for the past year and a half?*

The pipe didn't reappear on the other side of the shelves, so Lenny pressed his face against the cold brick wall, trying to see if it ended behind the unit with a tap. There was definitely something there, if only he could reach it.

Stretching out, Lenny managed to grab the item in his fingertips, but it wasn't the metal water tap that he expected to touch. It was a dusty paper tube, tied in the middle with a length of old black ribbon. He slid the tube towards him, pulling it free of the unit and holding it up to the dim light to examine it.

'Hey, lads!' he shouted. 'Come and see what I've found!' He turned to leave the room but, as he did so, he caught one of the legs of the shelves with his foot and the rusted metal snapped completely. The unit groaned and slowly began to topple forwards. Lenny leapt out and grabbed it from the front, managing to stop it at an impossible angle, the tools sliding dangerously close to the front of their shelves. Straining against the weight, he pushed it back against the wall and cautiously removed his hands, checking to see whether the unit was safe. It was, and he let out a long sigh.

Lenny turned to leave the room, and was almost at the door when the unit collapsed completely behind him, the deafening sound of tools crashing to the stone floor echoing around the cellar.

'Who's down there?' demanded a voice, accompanied by heavy footsteps hurrying down the staircase. Mr Wharpley! James dived into the main cellar with Lenny, Alexander switched off the light, and the trio just managed to duck behind the door before the furious caretaker appeared, torch in hand. He took one look at his scattered tools and sighed. 'Flippin' rust!'

he moaned, stooping to pick up the broken leg from the shelving unit. 'I *told* Tricky Ticky I needed some new shelves!'

The caretaker dropped to his knees and began to collect his tools carefully, checking them for chips or dents before laying them gently to one side. All the while he muttered about teachers getting new equipment when *they* needed it – why shouldn't he get a new shelving unit? After all, it was he who kept the place running day in, day out.

Behind him, James gestured for Alexander and Lenny to be quiet, then silently led the way out of the cellar and back up the stairs towards the welcoming daylight.

## CHAPTER 6
# THE BLUEPRINT

All the way through double maths, Alexander was itching to reach inside his rucksack, pull out the tube of paper and examine it. Still, as distractions went, complex algebra was up there with the best, and so he tackled the work with enthusiasm.

James, on the other hand, didn't find much comfort in equations. All he could think about was that Lenny had possibly stumbled upon the greatest clue to the cubicle four mystery so far. What could be written on the rolled-up paper?

Would it help them to understand what was going on in the girls' toilets? Or would it just complicate the situation more?

Glancing over his shoulder, James spotted Lenny staring out of the window, a troubled expression on his face. In a little over six minutes the bell would ring for break, and they would be able to find out what information the paper contained. Unless Alexander raised his hand and started asking questions, of course. James tried to grab his wrist and pull his arm back down, but Alexander simply raised his other hand. What was he doing now?

'Please, Mr Parker, what would you say were the most effective methods for dealing with algebraic manipulation?'

The maths teacher's face lit up. 'I'm so glad you asked that, Alexander, although the answer might take some time to explain . . .' The entire class groaned with frustration.

James and Lenny exchanged glances. The secrets of their find might have to wait longer than six minutes.

Had James and Lenny not been pacing impatiently behind the bike sheds, they might have noticed someone spying on them. He was a slight boy, thin almost to the point of being skeletal, and the shock of dirty blonde hair on top of his head gave him the look of a walking floor mop.

William Scroggins concentrated hard to stay in a form that appeared to be as solid as possible. His fact-finding mission would be over very soon indeed if one of the school pupils or staff discovered they could see right through him.

As Alexander arrived, weighed down with extra maths books, William tiptoed closer to eavesdrop on the conversation.

'Well, if it isn't Captain Pythagoras!' exclaimed Lenny as Alexander appeared.

'What do you mean?' came the reply.

'*Ten minutes!*' said Lenny. 'You kept us in maths for an extra *ten whole minutes* while Parker answered your question. Let me tell you, Stick, your popularity isn't exactly at its peak right now!'

'Some things are important!' countered Alexander. 'I was eager to discover whether the mechanics of probability had altered over the centuries.'

'Oddball,' muttered Lenny as he pulled a chocolate bar from his coat pocket and took a bite. James stepped between them.

'As fascinating as this conversation is,' he said, 'we've only got five minutes of break left. Where's the roll of paper?'

Alexander carefully piled his new textbooks on the ground and pulled the tube of paper from his rucksack. Taking a deep breath, he untied the knot in the black ribbon and unfurled the paper in his hands. James and Lenny craned to look.

The paper contained a detailed plan, with a neatly written heading above. 'Saint Sebastian's School, Grimesford,' read James aloud. 'Built on the site of the medieval plague pit.'

'P-plague pit?' stammered Lenny, gazing at the remains of his chocolate bar with disgust before tossing it aside. 'You mean, there are dead bodies underneath us, *right now*?'

'Well, statistically speaking there are bodies beneath you for much of your day,' droned Alexander. 'The bodies of previous generations weren't always buried in official graveyards.' Lenny rolled his eyes and sighed at the first sign of yet another history lesson. 'But, yes, if the school *is* built over a medieval plague pit, there will be plenty of dead bodies underneath us right now.'

James studied the plan. 'What *is* this?' he asked.

'It's a blueprint for the school,' answered Alexander. 'The original, Victorian building by the look of it.' He gestured to the largest room on the diagram. 'That will be what's the assembly hall these days.'

James shook his head in amazement as Alexander continued to point out individual rooms on the blueprint. Lenny, however, simply stared down at the ground, thinking hard.

'That's the cause of that weird stuff in the toilets,' he announced. James and Alexander looked up. 'The tentacle and the hand,' continued Lenny. 'It's the ghosts of the people buried beneath the school. They're trying to scare us off.'

'A ridiculous notion,' snorted Alexander. 'As I said earlier, the existence of spectral apparitions has yet to be conclusively proven.'

James looked at his friend. 'Do you have a better explanation for what's happening?'

Alexander thought for a second before replying, 'No. I don't.'

'So, what do we do?' asked Lenny.

'Contact *New Scientist*, or one of the other respected scientific journals!' exclaimed Alexander. 'If we've witnessed what I think we've witnessed, we could have convincing proof of a conscious afterlife! It's our duty!'

'All in good time, professor,' said James. 'But I was thinking more of what we can do to stop these things from terrorising the school.'

Alexander's face twisted into a mischievous grin – a sure sign that what was to come would be incredibly cheesy. 'I think we can all agree that it's a very *grave* situation!' he announced.

'Your jokes are terrifyingly bad!' said James.

'That's it! We could scare the ghosts off,' suggested Lenny.

'With his comedy?' asked James.

'No!' replied Lenny. 'Something else.'

'Attempt to scare those who frighten us?' mused Alexander. 'Turn the tables, as it were. A daring plan, to say the least. But how?'

'Well,' said Lenny, concentrating hard on the plan that was forming in his mind. 'If they died from the plague, they'll be scared of it. If we could make them think it's back – they might disappear and leave us alone.'

Alexander stared, open-mouthed. 'You want to recreate the Black Death in an effort to petrify its original victims?'

Lenny nodded. 'I rescued a rat I found trapped down a drain last week,' he explained. 'It's a scabby old thing: bits of fur missing, an eye infection and a big chunk out of its tail. With a bit of make-up, I reckon it could pass as a plague carrier. We just send it down into the sewers to stir things up a bit.'

'Are you still picking up stray animals and keeping them in your bedroom?' asked James.

'I keep the rat hidden in a box under my bed,' explained Lenny, 'along with a hedgehog that was attacked by a neighbour's dog, and a mole I found unconscious in the garden.'

'Your mum will go mental if she finds out,' said James.

'I say that's a risk worth taking,' said Alexander. 'The plan has merit.' He turned to Lenny. 'So, what do you call this repulsive beast?'

Lenny grinned. 'Whiskers!'

## CHAPTER 7
# THE WHOLE TRUTH?

William Scroggins skipped happily along the corridor outside the science rooms, singing to himself. This was turning out to be the best day of his afterlife.

He was just eleven years old when the plague had taken his life, and they hadn't been easy years. As soon as he'd been able to walk, he was put to work on his parents' farm. No school for William Scroggins. Until now.

Today he'd sat in on year seven's double maths lesson, even enjoying the extra ten minutes the boy called Alexander had added to the lesson. Year eight's French class was just as much fun, and he'd sat next to the prettiest girl he had ever seen. Stacey, she was called. Having never been taught to read, he hadn't been able to gather that from the cover of her exercise book, but another girl had called her that name while talking behind the teacher's back. Stacey. Stacey, Stacey, Stacey!

Of course, he'd had to change his appearance to go unnoticed by the other pupils. Even though he was technically the right age to be in those classes, his grubby, ragged clothes and the dark purple circles round his eyes would have caused him to stand out like a branded ox at a cattle fair. It was a simple matter of becoming completely transparent, one of the many tricks he'd learnt from his friend Ambrose since becoming a ghost.

While invisible, he'd also crept into the headmaster's office and watched as Mr Tick performed magic on a glowing box. 'Flipping computer' the box was called. At least, that's what Mr Tick had shouted at it when everything had stopped moving on the front of the box, and he'd had to pull out the black rope which attached it to the wall.

It would be a shame to lose all of these exciting experiences when the school closed down. Edith was very determined to see that happen and, even after she'd explained the purpose of William's visit to the surface, he hadn't really understood what the school's closure would mean. There was so much fun to be had up here.

So, William had decided not to tell Edith the truth. He wasn't going to lie to her, of course. That would be wrong. No, he was just going to tell her a little of what he had seen, and keep the rest to himself. If Edith wanted to know what the pupils were scared of, he'd tell her: not much.

He still wasn't sure what to do about the other problem, however: the three boys who had figured out the ghosts' existence, and who were planning to send a rat down into the sewers dressed up to make it look as though it was carrying the plague. That information he would keep to himself.

Arriving at the ground-floor girls' toilets, William glanced around to make sure he was alone, then turned himself invisible and slipped inside. There was no one about, so he dashed into cubicle four, slimmed his body down so that it looked like a string of spaghetti, and dived head first into the water.

He'd barely got past the U-bend when a long, thin arm appeared and its hand grabbed hold of his hair, dragging him through the pipes and into the sewers. It was Edith, of course. And Ambrose was with her.

'So?' she demanded as soon as he had reformed into the shape of a boy. 'What's

happening up there?' Her voice echoed noisily
throughout the network of brick tunnels.

William shrugged. 'Not much, really,' he said.
'A lot of the children have small stones tied to
bits of string which they push into their ears to
listen to someone called "empey three" and some
of them wear shoes that I think are made from
mice because they're white and they squeak
when they walk along the corridors . . .' He

paused to fix an image firmly in his mind. 'Oh, and there's one girl who's prettier than a lamb in springtime. She's called Stacey.'

Ambrose smiled at the soppy expression on William's face, but when Edith grabbed the boy's shoulders and shook him hard, he quickly turned it into a look of seriousness, in case she did the same to him.

'Never mind all that,' shouted Edith. 'How can we defeat them? What are their weaknesses?'

William thought hard. 'Erm, they don't like doing homework much.'

Edith pulled a face that either meant she was about to explode with rage, or that she badly needed the toilet. 'I meant, what are they *afraid* of?'

This was the moment William was dreading. He knew that Ambrose's appearance as the purple tentacle, and throwing the rotten, grey hand they'd borrowed from Bertram Ruttle's collection of body parts, had been the scariest thing these children had ever seen, but if he told Edith as much she'd have them haunting the classrooms from morning till night.

He glanced up at Ambrose for help, to discover that his friend had puffed out his cheeks and rolled his eyes back in his head. For a moment, William thought he might have gone mad but, when Ambrose raised his hands and clenched them into fists, he suddenly understood.

'The Gorilla!' he blurted. 'They're scared of the child they call "The Gorilla". He's a bully, and inflicts pain upon the smaller children if they don't do exactly what he says.'

Slowly, ever so slowly, a smile began to creep across Edith's face. Before long, she was cackling insanely and dancing around, her dirty skirt clutched in her bony fingers.

William looked back at Ambrose, who was watching Edith's dance with a horrified look on his face. Edith being happy could only mean one thing: she had a plan.

# CHAPTER 8
## RAT FANS

At 8.55 the following morning, Lenny carefully placed his school bag on to the desk, and gestured for James and Alexander to come over. After checking that no one else was watching, Lenny lifted a football shirt out of the bag and unwrapped it to reveal a small, home-made cage. James and Alexander crouched to peer at what was inside.

They found themselves faced with the most disgusting animal they had ever seen. The rat was covered with weeping sores, scars and

infected boils. James had to look away, but
Alexander simply stared.

'I thought you said he was just missing a bit
of fur,' he said.

'He is,' replied Lenny. 'The rest is just make-
up. Stacey came round to visit Leandra that
night, and I talked them into coming upstairs
to help me.'

James glared up at Lenny. 'Stacey Carmichael
was in your bedroom?'

Lenny nodded. 'For a couple of hours, yeah. That's her make-up all over Whiskers.'

Alexander laughed. 'Don't tell him that, you'll have him snogging the rat if he thinks he can get a taste of Stacey's lipstick!'

James kicked Alexander's shin. 'Shut up!' he hissed, blushing deeply.

'If I can drag you back to reality,' muttered Alexander as he rubbed his leg and frowned at his friend. 'We need a plan to get Whiskers here down into the sewers.'

James shrugged. 'I just figured we were going to flush him down the toilet in cubicle four.' He picked up the cage and stared at the rat inside. 'How long can he hold his breath for?'

Lenny snatched the cage from James and cradled it protectively. 'We are *not* flushing him down the toilet!' he said. 'It's bad enough that he has to suffer the indignity of being plastered in make-up.'

'Yeah, I bet he really hated lying in Stacey's lap while she pampered him for a couple of hours,' agreed Alexander.

As the bell rang for assembly, Lenny wrapped the cage up in his shirt again, and slipped it back inside his bag. It was going to be a long morning.

'The first letters from General Ned Ludd and the Army of Redressers were received by employers in Nottingham during the early months of eighteen-eleven,' droned Mr Hall, forty minutes into an already dragging second period of double history. As far as James and Lenny were concerned, he might as well have been talking about defusing thermo-nuclear devices. Assembly had been bad enough, but this was torture.

Even Alexander was fidgeting. His textbook remained closed for the first time in living memory. 'We've got to get back into Wharpley's workroom,' he whispered to James. 'I think I remember seeing a manhole cover in the floor which should lead to the sewers.'

'You *think* you saw a manhole cover?' replied James. 'You're not sure?'

'If you recall,' said Alexander, 'I was only in there for a second after Frankenstein back there had caused chaos with his size tens. I didn't have time to have a proper look around.'

'OK,' whispered James. 'We'll go down there at lunchtime and release the plague back into the pit.'

'Do you think the ghosts will fall for it?' asked Alexander.

James shrugged. 'Who knows what they'll do. But it's got to be worth a try. After all, what ghost in its right mind would want to be faced with the very disease that sent it to their grave?'

'Is this a private conversation, or can anyone join in?' boomed a voice.

Alexander looked up to see that Mr Hall, along with most of the class, was staring at their desk. 'I was, er, just explaining something about the Black Death of medieval times to James, sir,' he said, pleasantly.

Mr Hall nodded to his star pupil. 'As commendable as your interest in history is, Alexander, you are around four hundred years off the mark for today's lesson. We are discussing the machinery of the industrial revolution – something you would know if you had bothered to open your textbook!'

Someone sniggered as Alexander flicked through the book, trying to find the correct page. 'Yes, sir. Sorry, sir,' he mumbled as Mr Hall turned back to face the board.

'Now, the spinning jenny used a series of eight spindles as opposed to –'

'SQUEAK!'

Mr Hall turned round and glared at the sea of surprised faces that greeted him. 'What was that?' he demanded. No one seemed to know, as they were looking all around the room to find the source of the sound themselves.

James groaned. He knew exactly what it was, and a quick glance back at Lenny showed that his friend did, too. Lenny's eyes were shut tight, his school bag clamped tightly between his feet. James held his breath until Mr Hall turned his attention back to the board.

'As I was saying, the spinning jenny used eight spindles instead of one, and –'

'SQUEAK!'

Mr Hall spun round, his face red with rage. 'I distinctly heard a noise!' he shouted. 'And I demand to know what it is!'

Slowly, Lenny raised his hand.

'What's he doing?' hissed Alexander.

'No, please don't tell him. *Please* don't!' muttered James under his breath.

'Leonard?' said the history teacher. 'Do you know what's making that noise?'

James had his face buried in his hands.

Lenny nodded. 'Yes, sir,' he admitted. 'It was me.'

James looked up, amazed.

'You?' asked Mr Hall.

'Yes, sir,' repeated Lenny, his voice more confident now. 'I was making the sound of a spinning jenny.'

'A spinning jenny?' asked Mr Hall.

Lenny looked as though he might faint at any moment. 'I want to be a spinning *Lenny*,' he muttered, clearing his throat. 'Er, squeak! Squeak! Squeak!'

The class burst into laughter, all except for James and Alexander who breathed heavy sighs of relief.

Mr Hall stared at Lenny for a moment in disbelief, unsure what to say. 'OK,' he finally replied. 'Very good. But if you could keep the impressions to a minimum, we'll all get a lot more done.'

Shaking his head, Mr Hall turned back to the board and continued to write. 'Now, the spinning jenny . . .'

James turned in his chair in time to spot Lenny ripping apart a sandwich and pushing the pieces down into his bag, presumably trying to keep Whiskers more interested in food than in making noises.

The bell rang and chairs scraped across the floor as everyone jumped to their feet, eager for the fresh air of the playground. As Mr Hall barked out homework instructions, Lenny hoisted his bag to his shoulder and joined his friends.

'A spinning Lenny?' asked Alexander, dubiously.

'I couldn't think of anything else,' admitted Lenny.

'Well, at least he didn't find Whiskers,' said James. 'Come on. Let's get down to the cellar before anything else happens.'

He led the way from the classroom, past Mr Hall who patted Lenny on the shoulder. 'Is there anything you'd like to talk about, Leonard?' he asked.

Lenny shook his head. 'No, sir,' he said. 'I, er, just really like the technology of the early textile industry.' And, with that, he dashed out of the classroom, leaving his history teacher with what would easily prove to be the best staffroom anecdote of the week.

## CHAPTER 8
# WHARPLEY ON THE WARPATH

'He's down there,' said James as he, Lenny and Alexander listened at the door that led down to the cellar. The sound of an electric drill, and the strains of Elvis singing via a CD player could be heard faintly.

'What do we do now?' asked Lenny.

James shrugged. 'We'll have to try again tomorrow, if Mr Wharpley's not down there again, of course.'

Alexander shook his head. 'The ghosts could be on to us by then,' he said. 'In fact, they could be listening to what we're saying right now.'

Lenny looked up and down the corridor, nervously. 'Right now?' he asked.

'Of course,' replied Alexander. 'As spectral entities, they'll be more than adept at assuming translucence. The probability of an ectoplasmic encounter is extreme.'

'I wish you'd talk properly,' grumbled Lenny.

'He means that they can probably make themselves invisible,' said James. 'And they could be standing beside us at the moment.'

Lenny gingerly stretched out an arm and swept it back and forth through the air. 'You've just sliced some poor dead person's head off,' said Alexander, causing Lenny to wipe his hand repeatedly on his jumper.

'Stop winding him up!' ordered James. 'We have to get Whiskers into the sewers today. But how are we going to get down to that manhole cover if Wharpley's hanging around?'

'Simple,' replied Alexander. 'We enlist the help of the girls again.'

James turned to see Leandra and Stacey striding along the corridor.

'A spinning Lenny?' demanded Leandra as she arrived. Lenny blushed. Word certainly travelled fast around here. 'Do you know how much damage having a loony for a brother could do to my reputation?'

'Never mind that now,' interrupted Alexander. 'We have bigger fish to fry.' He smiled, wickedly. 'Or should that be lumpier soup to throw?'

Five minutes later, Stacey Carmichael was carefully pouring a bucket of vegetable soup over the floor of the hall, holding it at arm's length to try and avoid splashing her perfect

white trainers that she wore in place of her
ruined ballet pumps. She wasn't going to lose
another pair of shoes. The soup slopped noisily
on to the wooden floor.

James had started to ask why Alexander had a
spare key to the kitchens but, with the end of
break just minutes away, he figured it could wait
until later.

'Mr Wharpley!' screamed Leandra in as girly a voice as she could manage. 'It's *sooo* gross! Someone's just thrown up!'

James, Lenny and Alexander listened from inside the boys' toilets as the caretaker came thudding up the stairs clanking a bucket of sand. 'Lead the way,' he grunted, as Leandra set off on the longest route possible to the hall.

James signalled the all clear, and the three boys slipped out and back down to the cellar.

Elvis crooned on as James, Lenny and Alexander crept into Mr Wharpley's room as silently as they could manage.

'Over there,' whispered Alexander, pointing to the area behind a pile of broken desks. The rusted metal shelving unit had gone, and the tools were now piled into cardboard boxes around the room. James slid one of them across the floor to reveal a manhole cover, caked in dirt and black gunge.

'This should lead directly into the sewers if I'm following the old blueprint correctly,' said Alexander. 'All we have to do is lift it up and slip Whiskers down there to work his magic.'

'SQUEAK!' uttered Whiskers from deep inside Lenny's bag, as though accepting the mission.

James pushed his fingers into the foul-smelling goop that surrounded the manhole cover, and pulled as hard as he could, but it didn't budge. 'It's stuck!' he said.

'It's probably all this gunk around the edges,' explained Alexander. 'We'll need to shift it to have any chance of opening the manhole.'

Lenny checked his watch. 'There's only a couple of minutes left of break.'

'Then we'll remove what we can,' said James, 'and come back at lunchtime to send Whiskers down there.' He reached into a nearby cardboard box and pulled out three screwdrivers. Taking one each, Alexander and Lenny began to dig and scrape at the decades of mud and oil that held the manhole cover in place. James sighed heavily, and joined in.

The boys dug as hard and as fast as they could, spraying the goo all over themselves and the room. 'This stuff stinks,' muttered Lenny as another chunk of the gunk splattered on to his trousers.

'And little wonder,' said Alexander, pausing to wipe his sweating forehead. 'It will have been building up for years. In fact, I wouldn't be surprised if some of this material has oozed up from below the school and contains the original plague virus.'

Lenny and James dropped their screwdrivers with a clatter and scuttled away from the manhole. 'What's the matter?' asked Alexander, looking up.

'What's the matter?' shouted James. 'We've been digging up the Black Death for the past five minutes, and you want to know what's the matter?'

Alexander shook his head. 'The plague virus has been dead in Europe for about two hundred years!' he explained, smirking at the success of his joke. 'This stuff might stink, but it's completely harmless.' With that, he yanked his screwdriver

out of the mess and a lump of the muck flew up, hitting him squarely in the eye.

'*Argh!*' he squealed, throwing down his screwdriver and rubbing furiously at his face. James and Lenny shared a wry smile then got back to work, scraping away at the filthy goo once more.

Suddenly, everything went wrong.

'My tools!' thundered a voice. The boys looked up to see Mr Wharpley, at this moment the world's angriest school caretaker, standing over them. 'What are you doing with my tools?'

Alexander leapt to his feet. 'Mr Wharpley,' he began. 'It's not what it looks like. We've been asked to collect a sample of mud for our science lesson.'

'And you're using my best screwdrivers to do it?' roared the caretaker, snatching the tool from Alexander's hand and wiping it clean on his trouser leg. 'They were a present from my wife!'

James swallowed hard. If they could just calm Mr Wharpley down, they might get away with this. So long as no one said anything stupid.

'Well, she obviously hangs out with builders a lot, because she definitely knows her tools!' announced Alexander.

James hung his head, resigned to the punishment that was to come.

Just about everyone laughed as Mr Wharpley marched James, Lenny and Alexander through the school towards the headmaster's office. Talk of their plan had obviously spread too, as a group of year-nine boys began to sing the theme from *Ghostbusters* as they watched them go by. 'Who you gonna call?' shouted one of them.

Only Stacey and Leandra, who had witnessed the horrific events in the girls' toilets with them, stood silently as the three condemned pupils,

covered in dirt and mud from the cellar, were
paraded along the corridor.

James caught Stacey's eye; the girl of his dreams
seemed to be pitying him. But not 'I feel sorry for
you' pity. More like 'you sad little boy' pity.

James sighed and dragged his gaze away from
her. Things surely couldn't get any worse.

# CHAPTER 10
# WORSE

'I shall be calling your parents immediately!'
announced Mr Tick.

The headmaster had been extremely busy
when Mr Wharpley had barged into his office
moaning about 'three ruffians who had cruelly
ruined his entire collection of tools'.

He'd just placed a red nine on the black ten,
and was well on his way to an all-time solitaire
speed record. Of course, as soon as the caretaker
had appeared, Mr Tick had clicked a link that
replaced the game on the computer screen with

a very dull and official-looking spreadsheet. He couldn't have the staff thinking he was wasting his time.

'All right, Mr Wharpley, send them in,' he had sighed, gazing longingly at his keyboard, fingers itching to get back to the game.

The three boys trudged unhappily into the room and stood, heads hung low, in front of Mr

Tick's desk. The headmaster was dismayed to see his own son among the accused. This was going to take longer than he'd hoped, and the computer clock was still ticking away. The solitaire speed record, and his proud boasts about the result on his favourite Internet forum, Solitaire Isn't Just For Saddos, would have to wait until another day.

'I caught them digging up the floor of my workroom with my best tools,' exclaimed Mr Wharpley, determined to see the wrongdoers receive the maximum penalty the school rules would allow: expulsion.

'That will be all, Mr Wharpley,' announced the headmaster. 'I'll take it from here.'

'B–but, I want to make sure that –' spluttered the caretaker.

'I said, I'll take it from here!' instructed Mr Tick.

Mr Wharpley stomped out of the office, complaining under his breath about the treatment of manual workers in today's society. The door slammed behind him.

'We weren't digging up the floor, Dad,' said Alexander once the caretaker had gone.

Mr Tick raised a finger in his son's direction. 'You know the rules, Alexander,' he said. 'From nine o'clock in the morning to three-twenty in the afternoon I am *not* your father, I am your *headmaster.*'

Alexander groaned. 'OK, we weren't digging up the floor, *sir!*' he muttered.

A catchy jingle played from the computer speakers. The solitaire game was over; time had run out. Mr Tick sighed as he reached across to lower the volume. 'So, what were you doing down there?'

James and Lenny glanced at each other nervously, trying hard to think of an excuse for trespassing in the caretaker's room. But Alexander beat them to it.

'One of the year-nine kids knocked Lenny's football out of his hands, and it bounced down the stairs into Mr Wharpley's room,' he said. 'We went to retrieve it and, of course, to make sure it hadn't caused any damage.'

Mr Tick sat back in his chair, considering the answer. 'Then why did Mr Wharpley claim that you were digging into the floor with his tools?'

James was convinced that they had now been found out, but Alexander continued with his lies, undeterred. 'Once we found the football, we turned to leave. And that's when we heard the sound.'

'What sound?' asked Mr Tick. James and Lenny stared at Alexander. Yes, what sound?

'It sounded like crying,' Alexander continued, 'and we thought that maybe an animal had somehow fallen into the drains below the room and become stuck. So, we were trying to lift the manhole cover in the floor to see if we could rescue it. That's when Mr Wharpley discovered us.'

James shook his head. Where did Alexander get this stuff and, more importantly, why did he think it would wash with his father?

Mr Tick swivelled in his plush office chair, looking from dirty face to dirty face in front of him. 'And where is this football now?' he asked.

Alexander paled. 'E-excuse me?' he stammered.

'You said you went down to Mr Wharpley's room to retrieve a football,' said Mr Tick, calmly. 'Where is it now?'

*Say we couldn't find it*, thought James. *Say we couldn't find it.*

'It's in Lenny's bag!' announced Alexander. James wondered what the punishment would be for giving the headmaster's son a dead arm in front of him.

All eyes fell on Lenny's school bag that currently sat on a chair at the side of the desk.

Mr Tick got to his feet and lifted the bag on to his desk. Slowly, he dragged the zip back and slid his hand inside the holdall.

'SQUEAK!'

The noise caused the headmaster to pull his hand back out of the bag in horror. 'What's in there?' he demanded. This time, even Alexander didn't have an answer. 'I asked what is in there!' roared the headmaster. The boys all stayed silent.

'Empty the contents of the bag on to my desk!'
commanded Mr Tick, keeping his own hands
clear of the bag. He'd never beat the solitaire
record if he found himself missing a couple
of fingers.

James watched miserably as Lenny placed a
pile of textbooks down in front of the
headmaster. He'd have to produce Whiskers next,
and the boys would then go down in history as
the first pupils ever to be expelled for bringing
the Black Death into school.

Lenny dropped his pencil case on to the desk
and then hesitated, reluctant to take the cage
containing Whiskers out of his bag.

'I shall be calling your parents immediately,'
announced Mr Tick, 'if you do not empty that
bag right *now*!'

Sighing, Lenny reached inside for Whiskers.

At that moment, the door to the office
slammed open. Everyone spun round, half

expecting to see the enraged caretaker again, but instead they found themselves faced with the headmaster's secretary, Miss Keys.

'He's missing!' she blurted out, breathlessly. 'He hasn't been seen since this morning!'

Mr Tick darted round his desk and led his secretary to a chair, helping her to sit. 'Calm down, woman,' he ordered. 'You're hysterical.' Miss Keys grabbed the remainder of the headmaster's cup of tea that had gone cold while he'd been concentrating on where to place that red queen, and gulped it down in one.

'Now, who's missing?' demanded Mr Tick, taking the 'Solitaire Champ' mug from her trembling hands before anything untoward happened to it.

'Gordon Carver!' announced Miss Keys. James, Lenny and Alexander exchanged glances at the news. 'He didn't turn up for PE, and no one's seen him since registration!' added the secretary.

Mr Tick remained composed. 'The Carver boy has been known to skip lessons before, Miss Keys. Have you checked with the boy's parents?'

Miss Keys nodded furiously. 'He's not at home, either. And no one saw him leaving the school grounds!'

Mr Tick turned to the boys who remained motionless before his desk. 'Out!' he commanded.

'But, Dad –,' began Alexander, stopping only when James nudged him painfully in the ribs.

'I said, get out!' shouted the headmaster. 'You too, Miss Keys!'

The boys grabbed the contents of Lenny's bag and followed the secretary out of the office.

As the door closed behind them, Mr Tick dropped unhappily back into his chair. A missing pupil; that's all he needed. Personally, he didn't much care for Gordon Carver, or indeed for any of the other pupils at the school. But a missing pupil could mean he'd lose his job.

There was no way he would be able to afford his annual trip to the Norwich Solitaire Convention if that happened.

## CHAPTER 11
# A TENTS SITUATION

Lenny leant back against the wall behind the bike sheds with a sigh, pulling a packet of crisps from his pocket and opening it. 'What do you reckon's happened to The Gorilla?' he asked through a mouthful of salt and vinegar.

'He's just decided he's got better things to do than go to classes,' replied James.

'Well, *we* haven't!' said Alexander, checking his watch. 'It's already over halfway through English. We'll get there in time to collect our homework if we set off now.'

Lenny glanced up at his friend. 'Have you ever wondered why you get bullied so much?' he asked, stuffing another handful of crisps into his mouth.

'There's no reason to victimise another pupil simply because they appreciate a solid education,' claimed Alexander.

'Well, Gordon Carver obviously thinks there is,' said James. 'That is, if he isn't being torn limb from limb by vile, supernatural creatures at this very moment.'

Lenny sighed and threw his bag of crisps into a dustbin. 'I'm never eating near you two again,' he groaned.

'Which brings us back to our current problem,' said Alexander. 'How are we going to get Whiskers into the sewer now?'

'We can't go back to Mr Wharpley's workroom,' answered James. 'If he catches us in there again, he'll be calling for the death

101

penalty.' He thought for a second. 'There must be another way down there. Where's that blueprint?'

'In my locker,' said Alexander.

Lenny and James peered over Alexander's shoulders as he unrolled the plan of the old school, shielding the precious document from the other pupils who filled the corridors on their way to get lunch.

'There!' said James, pointing to a small, neatly drawn section to the left of the school. 'That's another opening into the sewers.'

Alexander slammed his locker door and led the way along the corridor to the area specified on the drawing. If this was indeed another entrance to the sewer system, he hoped it would be easier to access than the one down in the cellar.

'It's just outside what's now the history classroom,' he said, glancing briefly at the plan again. The sight of Alexander doing school work at lunchtime was nothing out of the ordinary, and so no one gave him a second glance.

'Outside the history room?' asked Lenny as they stepped out into the fresh air, and turned the corner. 'Isn't that . . .'

'The staff car park!' finished James glumly as the trio came to a halt. He dropped to his knees and studied the tarmac. He spotted another manhole cover – the entrance to the sewers they needed – currently lying underneath Mr Tick's car.

'What now?' he asked.

'Camping?' repeated James's dad that evening. 'It's a bit short notice, isn't it?'

'Well, it *is* Friday,' explained James. 'There's no school tomorrow. We just thought we'd do something a bit different.'

'Whose garden are you putting the tents up in?' asked his mum. What was this? Quiz night?

'We're staying at Dave's,' James lied, as calmly as he could, wishing he had Alexander's skill at telling untruths.

'Dave?' said his mum. 'Who's Dave?'

'You know Dave!' gushed James, wiping his already sweating palms on his trousers. 'Tall lad, brown hair. Lives on Mire Street, near the school.'

'I'm not sure that I –' began his mum before being interrupted by his father.

'He's making friends!' said his dad, proudly. 'Not an easy task when you've just moved to a new area.' He turned to face his son. 'I'll drop you off after tea,' he promised, ruffling James's hair.

James smiled sweetly. The family had only moved to Grimesford after his dad had lost his job, and now he was trying hard to make the transition as easy as possible for them. 'Thanks, Dad,' said James.

Two hours later, carrying a two-man tent and a rucksack filled with sandwiches and diet cola, James was dropped off at a house in Mire Street, down the road from St Sebastian's. Lenny and Alexander were already there, in the front garden, waiting for him.

'I think I'd better go and talk to the boy's mother,' said Mrs Simpson, as the car halted.

'She's, er . . . out shopping!' exclaimed James quickly. 'I'll get her to give you a ring if she needs to speak to you!' With that, he jumped out of the car, slammed the door and stood with Alexander and Lenny, waving frantically.

'See you in the morning!' he shouted, a little too enthusiastically. Shrugging, James's mum nodded to his dad, and the car pulled away. The boys didn't stop waving until it had turned the corner, and was out of sight.

'I thought they'd never leave!' sighed James.

Lenny nodded. 'My dad was like that, too.'

'My dad's been on the phone all night to Gordon's parents,' said Alexander. 'Gordon still hasn't turned up. They were thinking of calling the police when I left.'

Behind him, the hall light of the house came on and the front door was jerked open by a grumpy-looking, middle-aged woman. 'Who are you lot?' she demanded.

Alexander smiled politely. 'We're Boy Scouts on the lookout for persons in need of our help.'

The woman growled. 'Oh, yeah?' she said. 'And who do you think I am?'

'That's easy,' replied James. 'You're Dave.'

As the sun began to disappear behind the science lab, the boys arrived at the school gates and swung them noiselessly open. Thank goodness Mr Wharpley had stuck to his usual habit of forgetting to lock them.

James led the way across the deserted car park, the beam of his torch cutting through the darkness. 'There it is,' he whispered, lighting up the manhole cover, now freed of the vehicle that had sat above it all day.

Kneeling, James and Alexander ran their fingers around the edge of the metal cover until they found places to grab hold. Straining against the weight, they lifted the cover off, revealing a pitch-black chasm below.

Lenny reached into his bag and carefully lifted out Whiskers, who seemed to be glad of the fresh air. He held the heavily made-up rat to his face and scratched it behind the ear.

James looked from Alexander to Lenny and back again. 'Ready?' he asked.

## CHAPTER 12
# BULLY BAITING

Gordon 'The Gorilla' Carver struggled to free himself from the ropes that tied him firmly to the old, broken school chair. His legs splashed about wildly in filthy, brown water that swirled up to his knees, containing lumps of something he didn't dare think about. It couldn't really be that, could it?

He was in some kind of underground cave, lit by an eerie glow that seemed to flicker constantly. And he had the strangest sensation that he was being watched, that thousands of pairs of eyes were on him at that very moment, as though he was the exhibit at some ghastly freak show.

*And here's that vile woman again,* he thought. *Why can't she just leave me alone? I'll be good. Promise. Just let me go back home. Please!*

Edith danced merrily through the puddles of raw sewage towards Gordon, cackling crazily. 'How's my little pet?' she sang, circling the bully and running her bony fingers through his hair. 'Ready for his makeover?'

Behind her, Ambrose and William watched with expressions of concern. They knew that Gordon had been nasty to a lot of people, but he didn't deserve anything like this.

Ambrose opened his mouth to object to the scene in front of him, but suddenly found his mouth filled with Edith's hand as she reached down his throat to grab a recently swallowed leech. He gagged.

'Come to Mama, my pretty,' she oozed as
she held the wriggling leech up to the dim
light before laying it carefully on to Gordon's
face. 'Stick on, little creature. Suck the face of
your host!'

Gordon screamed in horror as the leech
slithered over his skin.

Edith laughed and clapped her hands. Her
plan was coming together perfectly. If the pupils
of St Sebastian's were scared of The Gorilla in his

everyday, human form, just *imagine* how they'd react when they saw what he would look like after her handiwork.

She raised her hands to the amphitheatre and shouted, 'Reveal yourselves, my friends. Introduce yourselves to our guest!' Gordon watched in terror as hundreds of men, women and children melted into view from the shadows, each one covered in buboes from the Black Death, warts and sores.

They paraded past him, smiling and bowing politely. Every now and again, Edith would pluck a scab from one of the faces, or rip a bubo from an armpit and attach it to Gordon's own body. Before long, the bully looked as though he had perished from the plague himself. He struggled violently against the ropes that were cutting painfully into his arms.

'Calm yourself, my lovely!' cooed Edith, leaning down to plant a wet kiss on Gordon's cheek. 'We have all weekend to get to know each other and, when Monday comes around, the children above us will run screaming from the monster that is – *you*!'

She raised her hands above her head in a victory salute that brought a thunder of applause from the assembled ghosts and ghouls.

Gordon was sobbing now, his salty tears burning the wounds that covered his face. This *had* to be a nightmare. He would wake up at any moment. *Please* let him wake up! This couldn't be real.

And then he saw the rat.

The ghosts didn't notice Whiskers at first. They were too busy dancing with joy at the thought of St Sebastian's School being be no more to spot one little rodent. Even Edith didn't think to look down, until she heard the noise from the lid of her upturned barrel.

'SQUEAK!'

Silence invaded the cavern. One by one, the ghosts focused on the rat. The rat that looked like no other they had seen for over six hundred years. The rat that was clearly carrying the Black Death.

'Oh, no,' muttered William a split second before utter chaos broke out.

Screaming and shouting, the ghosts clambered over each other, fighting to get away from the disease which had brought them a disgusting, pain-wracked death centuries before. They bit, kicked and scratched anyone who got in their way, desperate to be free of the plague.

'No, wait!' shouted William in vain. 'It's just a pet rat they put make-up on! And it can't hurt us anyway – we're already dead, remember?' But his voice was lost in the screams that echoed around the cavern.

Even Edith had lost control. 'I won't go through that again!' she screamed, pushing

Gordon's chair over in an effort to escape. 'Get it away from me!'

His face hit the top of the barrel as the chair toppled forwards, his eyes just centimetres from the bewildered rat.

'SQUEAK!'

Gordon fainted, sinking happily into blackness as Whiskers licked at the bully's nose.

'We have to stop them!' shouted William to
Ambrose, who was frozen to the spot with fear.
'It's just a trick!' Ambrose said nothing, his gaze
fixed on the rat. William reached up and slapped
him hard across the face. 'Ambrose!' he screamed.
'Help me!'

Ambrose Harbottle nodded, and the two ghosts
dashed into the centre of the spectral riot. Things
had really got out of hand now as the exit tunnels
had become blocked with the terrified dead.

Lady Grimes had paled even further than
usual, having lost her usual air of refinement,
clawing madly at any ghost that dared to get in
her way.  ·

Bertram Ruttle had grabbed the nearest
skeleton he could find, and was swinging it
around to try and clear a path to freedom. Each
time the skull connected with a ghostly head, he
clambered over the fallen spook and took aim at
the next terrified phantom.

The Headless Horseman had pulled his head from beneath his arm, and was holding it out so that it could bite at other ghosts' bottoms, making them think the rat had caught up with them.

William found Edith in a corner of the amphitheatre, crouched behind an old, crumbling gravestone, rocking back and forth. 'Edith, listen to me!' he commanded. 'This isn't real! None of it is real! You have to speak to them. They'll listen to you!'

Edith, however, was far from with it, having withdrawn inside her mind to her 'happy place': the ramshackle hut where she had lived all those years ago, merrily picking on her useless lump of a husband. *You waste of skin!* she shouted at him, deep in her unconscious. *Don't come back until you've caught something for dinner!*

'SQUEAK!'

William spun round. 'We have to get that rat out of here!' he shouted to Ambrose, who was busy trying to fight his way out from underneath Lady Grimes, who had fainted on top of him the moment the Headless Horseman's teeth had sunk into her behind.

William leapt over Edith and raced for Whiskers, who was still sitting calmly on top of the barrel, unaware of the chaos he had caused. The boy ducked as Bertram Ruttle swung a length of spine violently past his head, all that was left of his skeletal weapon. 'Almost there,' said William to himself. 'Just a few more metres.'

He reached the barrel and pulled Gordon's chair upright. The bully slumped back in the seat, still deep in a faint. As William stretched out his hand to pick up the rat, a skull flew out of the pack of fighting ghosts and collided with the boy's head.

The last thing William heard as he sank to his knees was a tiny voice off to his left: 'Hey, that's me!'

## CHAPTER 13
# SKY HIGH

James lay on his stomach on the tarmac and peered down inside the pipe that led to the sewers. The torch was doing little, if anything, to relieve the darkness.

'Can you see him?' asked Lenny, hopefully.

'Who?' James's voice echoed eerily from the sewer entrance.

'Whiskers!' replied Lenny. 'Can you see Whiskers anywhere?'

Alexander shone his torch into Lenny's face. 'He'll be long gone by now,' he said.

'What?' muttered Lenny, trying hard to stop his bottom lip from trembling.

'He's a rat, Lenny,' said Alexander. 'We've released him down into the sewers, where he's surrounded by his own kind. I doubt you'll be seeing him again.'

'He's not coming back?' asked Lenny, his eyes filling with tears.

Alexander shook his head. 'What did you think he was? A homing rat?'

'I just didn't realise,' mumbled Lenny as he wiped away his tears. 'I just thought he'd come back ...'

James lifted his head out of the hole and sat up. 'It's OK,' he said, gently. 'When this is all over, we'll go down there and look for him. You never know, we might –' he stopped, suddenly aware of a distant rumbling noise coming from underground. 'Can you guys hear that?' he asked.

The noise grew in volume, sounding now like the howl of a strong wind. It was coming from the sewers.

James, Alexander and Lenny leant over the hole, their torches aimed down into the darkness. The noise was a deafening roar now. Something was approaching.

The boys were thrown on to their backs as thousands of ghosts erupted through the manhole and fled up into the air. Slime and sewage rained down as men, women and children raced upwards, screaming in terror at what they had just witnessed.

James lay back on the ground, mouth open in astonishment at the scene he was witnessing. The ghosts whirled around each other, jostling for position as the surge of spirits raced for the clear night sky.

'Ghosts!' mouthed Lenny, staring upwards. 'Th-they're real.'

122

'And they're scared,' added Alexander. 'We've done it. They're leaving!' He looked from James to Lenny, grinning madly. 'We did it!'

Soon, the sky was a writhing, swirling mass of spirits. Tortured faces appeared and disappeared among the pulsating mass. Screams echoed into the night.

After a moment, the sky above the school seemed to glow, a flickering light that spread quickly through the collection of ghosts. It grew brighter and brighter – greens, reds and blues shooting from one spectre to another. Then, with a massive boom, the cloud of phantoms exploded, sending trails of light shooting across the sky.

James, Lenny and Alexander lay still, trying to catch their breath.

The first thing William Scroggins noticed when he came round was the wind whistling past his face. He opened his eyes to find himself high above the school, carried along by a flood of ghosts that were screaming up into the cold night air. Something flew past him, knocking into his hand as it sped downwards.

'SQUEAK!'

The rat! The rat that had started it all. By rights, he should let it fall back to earth and hit the ground hard. It had caused chaos among the plague-pit ghosts, scaring them enough to flee the sewers that had been their home for the past six hundred years.

But he knew the rat was a pet, a friend to the largest of the three boys who had planned this. William knew what it was like to need a friend, so he forced himself round and, pressing his feet against the belly of a particularly large ghost, launched himself down towards the carpark.

He caught up with the rat quickly and managed to grab its tail. It spun round in the air,

teeth bared, but calmed down when it saw the
kind expression on the boy's face.

'It's OK,' said William, soothingly. 'I've got
you.' Then a thought struck him. If the rat had
been thrown up here with the ghosts, perhaps
the bully had been, too. He searched the
screaming crowd for a familiar face and spotted
Ambrose, trying to free himself from Edith's
terrified clutches.

'Ambrose!' he yelled, desperate to make himself
heard about the noise. His friend looked up and
saw him. 'The boy!' shouted William. 'Find the
boy!' Ambrose nodded and forced his way deep
into the seething mass of ghostly bodies.

William concentrated hard for a moment to
make himself invisible, then continued downwards.

Lenny clambered to his feet, wiping furiously
at the mud and dirt that had rained down

upon them. 'Hey! What's that?' he heard
Alexander say.

Lenny looked up to see a dark object falling
towards them. Oh, no, not another ghost . . .

'SQUEAK!'

'Whiskers!' shouted Lenny, and held up his
hands to try and catch his pet. The rat changed
direction as a gust of wind caught it and Lenny
dashed across the car park towards it. He tripped
over the discarded manhole cover and crashed to

126

the ground. There was no way he was going to reach Whiskers now; the rat would hit the tarmac right in front of him.

But, at the last moment, Whiskers changed direction again and landed safely in Lenny's outstretched hands.

'Incredible!' muttered Alexander as he watched Lenny cuddle and kiss his pet.

Unseen by everyone but the rat itself, William Scroggins let go of its tail and smiled.

'Help me!' screamed a voice from above the boys. James looked up to see a large but familiar shape hurtling back towards the ground.

'The Gorilla!' he shouted, grabbing Alexander's hands to form a cradle. Lenny pushed Whiskers into his school bag and rushed over to join them.

Positioning themselves below the falling bully, the boys leant back, bracing themselves for the impact. High above them, an invisible Ambrose Harbottle tugged hard at The Gorilla's hair, trying desperately to slow his fall. When Gordon landed, James, Alexander and Lenny collapsed heavily on top of him. The Gorilla quickly leapt to his feet, terrified but unhurt.

'Where is she?' he screamed, pulling the leech from his face. 'The one with the laugh! Keep her away from me!'

James glanced around the playground. 'There's no one else here,' he said. 'Just us.'

Gordon tried his best to pull himself together. 'R-right!' he stammered, pointing at each boy in turn. 'Don't you tell anyone about this!'

Alexander stepped up to face him. 'What's in it for us?' he asked.

'I'll . . . I'll leave you alone!' Gordon replied. 'Just keep this quiet.' And then he ran off across the car park, muttering to himself about ghosts, ghouls and raw sewage.

James took a deep breath, bending down to drag the cover back over the manhole. 'I don't

128

know about you two,' he said, straightening up.
'But, I'm ready for bed.'

Smiling, Alexander and Lenny gathered their
bags and joined their friend as he headed for the
school gates and home.

William and Ambrose watched the three boys
walk away. 'I guess things are going to be a little
quieter around here from now on,' said Ambrose,
cheerfully.

A hand clamped down hard on to his shoulder.
'That's what *you* think,' cackled a voice. Edith
Codd grinned wickedly as she transformed
herself, William and Ambrose into vapour,
dragging the two ghosts down through the
cracks in the manhole cover and back into
the sewer below.

'I thought we'd finished with the school!'
Ambrose's voice echoed up into the night air.

'That's just where you're wrong!' cackled
Edith. 'We haven't even begun!'

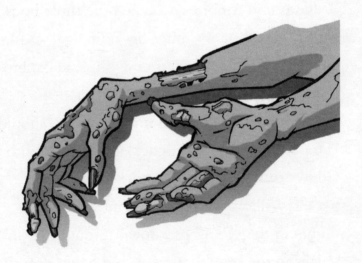

**SURNAME:** Simpson

**FIRST NAME:** James

**AGE:** 11

**HEIGHT:** 1.6 metres

**EYES:** Hazel

**HAIR:** Mousy brown and scruffy

FACT FILE

**LIKES:** Gaming, skateboarding, sports, Stacey (although he'd die rather than admit it)

**DISLIKES:** Homework, sitting still for any length of time, wearing his school tie

**SPECIAL SKILL:** Getting sent to Mr Tick's office; persuading Lenny and Alexander to investigate the spooky goings-on at St Sebastian's

**INTERESTING FACT:** James joined St Sebastian's later than the other year sevens. This was because his family relocated to Grimesford a term in to the new school year when his dad moved job

For more facts on James Simpson, go to **www.too-ghoul.com**

# Is Your Toilet Haunted?

## Answer these questions to find out ... you could be in danger!

**1** **Which of these best describes your toilet?**

a. Clean, pristine and shiny
b. A few skid marks, wonky seat, a bit whiffy
c. Covered in black gunge and acidic green goo

**2** **What noise does your loo make when you flush it?**

a. A splashing, watery noise
b. A clunk and a gurgle
c. A deafening, spine-chilling roar

**3** **How does your toilet smell?**

a. It smells of flowers and perfume
b. A bit stinky after Dad's used it, but OK
c. So bad that the paint has been stripped off the door

FOR MORE QUIZZES, VISIT **www.too-ghoul.com**

**4 When you sit on your loo, what can you feel?**

**a.** The cold seat, and that's about it
**b.** The loo-roll holder pressing against your arm
**c.** Something slimy curling round your leg

**5 Have any of the following ever gone missing down your loo?**

**a.** Your baseball hat when it fell down there
**b.** A marble that dropped out of your pocket
**c.** Several of your friends

**6 How can you tell if someone else is using your loo?**

**a.** There's an 'engaged' sign on the door
**b.** You can hear your dad singing while he's sitting on it
**c.** The whole house shakes and you can hear a terrible screaming noise

## How did you score?

**Mostly As**: You have a lovely, safe toilet. You should visit it more often.

**Mostly Bs**: You have a normal loo, but beware of any changes . . .

**Mostly Cs**: You'd better not be reading this on the toilet. **IT'S HAUNTED!**

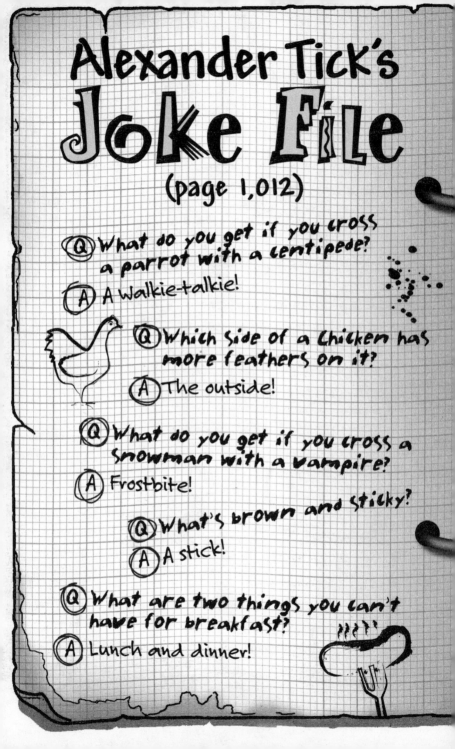

# Rat Phrase book

## by Whiskers

### *Learn to speak rodent in one easy lesson!*

| | |
|---|---|
| **Squeak** | Hello |
| **Squeak** | Goodbye |
| **Nibble** | Please feed me |
| **Nibble, nibble** | I'm bored with this maths lesson now |
| **Squeak, squeeeeak** | I really don't want any make-up on, thanks |
| **Nibble, nibble, squeak** | Actually, I don't mind if you put it on me, Stacey. Do you want to go to the cinema sometime? I'm considered quite handsome in the rat world, you know |
| **Squeak, squeeeeak, nibble, squeak** | I don't think you should blame us rats for the Black Death. It was all those pesky fleas' fault |
| **Nibble, squeak, nibble** | There's no way I'm going down that toilet. Even rats have standards! |
| **Squeaksqueaksqueaksqueak!** | What am I doing down in this pit? I think I prefer my cage |
| **Squeeeeeeeeeeeeeeeeeak!** | Help! I'm falling out of the sky in a cloud of ghosts! |

Can't wait for the next book in the series?
Here's a sneak preview of

# THE BUBONIC BUILDERS

available now from all good bookshops,
or **www.too-ghoul.com**

# CHAPTER 1
## TOILET TALES

'But I need to *go*!' Alexander wailed, dancing from foot to shiny-shoed foot. It was break time, and the corridors of St Sebastian's were crammed with pupils. All the teachers were tucked safely away in the staffroom, slurping coffee.

'Well, go then, Stick! What's your problem?' asked James, pulling the sagging knot in his tie even looser.

'You know – girls!'

'Sorry – I don't get the connection. It's not one of your terrible jokes coming on, is it?'

138

'Looks like something'll be coming soon – a puddle!' sneered Gordon 'The Gorilla' Carver – the school bully – as he scooted past, clipping Alexander round the back of the head.

James glared after the bully as he ran down the corridor. 'Stick – I hate to say this, but The Gorilla has a point. You'd better go now!'

'But . . . it's all of these girls invading our conveniences. It's very *in*convenient! You go rushing in, unzipping your fly, and a girl's there doing girly stuff like brushing her manky hair or something – and she looks at you like you're the *contents* of the toilet instead of just being there because you need to use it . . .' Alexander groaned.

'Well, you can't really blame them, you know,' said Lenny. 'There's only one set of girls' loos left for all the girls in the entire school while their ground-floor block is being rebuilt.'

At that moment, Leandra Maxwell, Lenny's sister, arrived. Stacey Carmichael, her best friend and the prettiest girl in school, trailed in her wake.

'New dance, Stick?' she honked. 'Very nice. Not sure it'll catch on though. Is it The Widdle Waltz? Or The Tinkle Tango?'

'It's not funny, Leandra!' growled Lenny. He shared his sister's dark curly hair and deep brown eyes, but that's where the similarities ended. Leandra liked to tease. Her brother Lenny was the kindest person ever.

'You . . . you should keep out of our lavatories – it's against school rules!' Alexander blustered.

By now, a small crowd had begun to gather. Girls screeched with laughter and even a few boys were grinning. The Gorilla arrived, smelling trouble.

'Oh, yes – and *Daddy*'s the headmaster, isn't he? He'd be cross if we broke his precious rules, wouldn't he?' The Gorilla snarled, snapping a bubblegum bubble in Alexander's face. Even the sugary smell couldn't sweeten his mean expression. Lenny pushed the bully away.

'Leave him alone, Carver!'

'Who are you pushing about?' the bully blustered. 'If I could be bothered, I'd have you . . .' he sneered at Lenny. 'You're only friends with that loser,' he jabbed Alexander in the chest with a chubby finger, 'because you like hopeless cases! I saw you, carrying that stupid hedgehog with scorched prickles you rescued last week.'

He turned to the crowd. 'He's got it in his
locker, y'know. It smells, *and* it's full of fleas.'
He turned back to Alexander and poked him
in the shoulder. 'Yeah – just like you, Stick!
And from the look of you, you're about to get
even smellier!'

Alexander looked away.

Lenny got closer to Gordon. 'I said, leave . . .
him . . . alone!' he growled.

Leandra stepped in between the boys.

A small girl tugged at Leandra's arm. 'Hey,
you know, I wouldn't like to use the boys' toilets.
I heard they were haunted . . .' she said. Leandra
turned and frowned at the girl and she let go,
smoothing the older girl's jumper sleeve.
Continuing bravely, she added, 'Really. I heard
that a kid went into that loo . . . and never came
out again!'

'I heard that zombies ate him,' a boy grimaced
horribly.

Stacey gave a pretty little shudder that made her short skirt twitch. It made a few of the boys twitch, too, like a chain reaction.

'Well, I heard there's an alien octopus that lives down the pipes. It eats poo – and year sevens!' a boy in year nine added.

'Naw . . . a headless horseman sweeps through the toilets banging on doors with his sword and slicing off legs at the ankles – knickers and all!' his friend called, swishing the air with an imaginary sabre as he spoke.

'Well,' Leandra said drily, 'I don't suppose many boys are sat there constipated with all that going on!' Stacey covered her mouth with her hand, her pink glossy nails sparkling as she tittered.

'I heard it was a portal for a dump demon,' said a tall year eight. 'It feeds off the gases in the toilets and suffocates people with its stinky breath as they sit on the throne. Its victims are

143

doomed to haunt the toilet forever, wafting around on a cloud of methane . . .'

'From the stink coming out of the boys' toilets, I can believe *that* story!' laughed Leandra.

'I heard there's a vampire toilet seat in one of the cubicles,' another boy whispered. 'You sit down quite happily, but you notice that the seat's deathly cold. Just as it starts to warm up and you get comfy – CHOMP! Spiky gnashers clamp down on your bum. You're stuck there until every drop of your blood is drained – and you're dead!'

'Or should that be *undead*?' laughed another boy, sweeping his jacket over his shoulders like a vampire's cloak. Snapping his teeth at the crowd, he made a beeline for Stacey and her delicate pink neck. Leandra raised a hand in front of his face and the boy stopped dead. He melted into the crowd again.

'No – you're all wrong. It's a ghoul that hides in the shadows and snatches kids as they flush

– and the noise hides their screams,' a small, worried boy said with a shudder.

'Actually, it's The Toilet Man,' a year-nine boy said, leaning against the wall. 'You say his name three times as you look in the mirror and your reflection slowly changes. Smoke swirls around your face and your eyes glint gold, like snake eyes. You bend closer to the mirror for a better look, rubbing it with your hand . . .' Everyone leant in as the boy told his tale.

'And The Toilet Man *grabs* it with his scaly talons and pulls you in!' he shouted, catching Stacey's hands and tugging her towards him. Everyone jumped.

'Well, that one's enough to make you wet yourself!' James laughed, suddenly reminded of Alexander's problem. He was now red in the face and quite obviously in pain, clutching the strap of his backpack so tightly that his knuckles were white.

'Come on, Stick,' Lenny whispered to his friend, 'while they're busy here, you can go to the loo undisturbed. I'll be your lookout and check for sneaky girls.' Alexander smiled gratefully. Lenny glowered at Gordon once more as they left.

'If only they all knew how close to the truth their stories are,' James sighed to himself as he made his way off down the corridor.